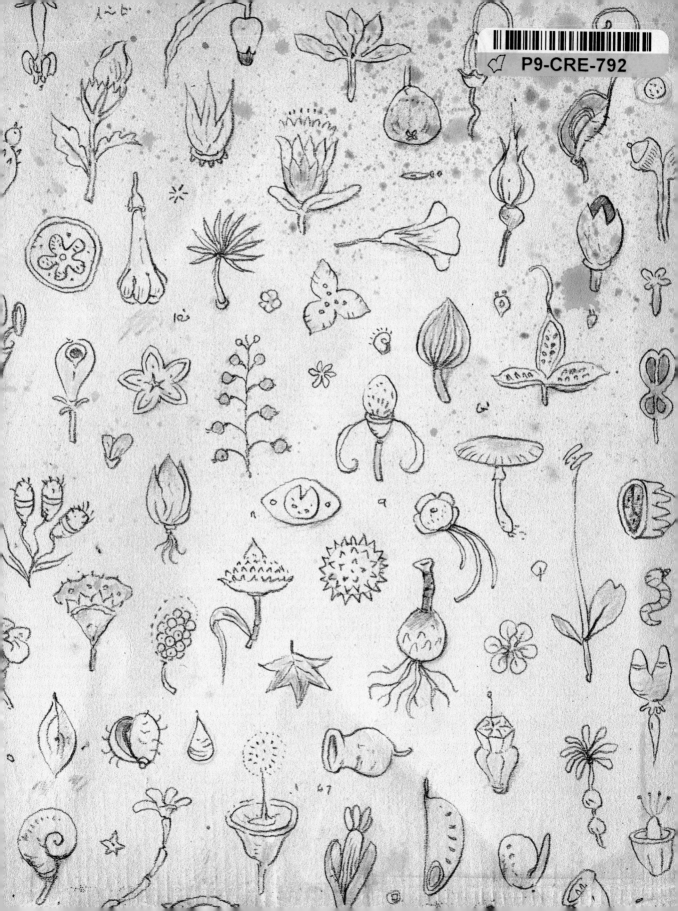

eric

eric

shaun tan

SCHOLASTIC PRESS
NEW YORK

ERIC

Some years ago we had a foreign exchange
student come to live with us. We found it very difficult
to pronounce his name correctly, but he didn't
mind. He told us to just call him "Eric."

We had repainted the spare room, bought
new rugs and furniture, and generally made sure
everything would be comfortable for him. So I can't say
why it was that Eric chose to sleep and study most
of the time in our kitchen pantry.

"It must be a cultural thing," said Mum.
"As long as he is happy."

We started storing food and kitchen things in other
cupboards so we wouldn't disturb him.

But sometimes I wondered if Eric was happy;
he was so polite that I'm not sure he would have
told us if something bothered him.

A few times I saw him through the pantry door gap,
studying with silent intensity, and imagined what it
might be like for him here in our country.

Secretly I had been looking forward to having a foreign visitor —
I had so many things to show him. For once I could be a local
expert, a fountain of interesting facts and opinions. Fortunately,
Eric was very curious and always had plenty of questions.

Unfortunately, they weren't the kind of questions I had been
expecting. Most of the time I could only say, "I'm not really sure"
or "That's just how it is." I didn't feel very helpful at all.

I think Eric enjoyed these trips, but it was hard to really know. He just didn't say very much.

Most of the time he seemed only interested
in small things he discovered on the ground. I might
have found this a little exasperating, but kept
thinking about what Mum had said.

About the cultural thing.

Then I didn't mind so much.

Even so, none of us could help but be bewildered by the way Eric left our home: a sudden departure early one morning, with little more than a wave and a polite goodbye.

It actually took us a while to realize he wasn't coming back.

There was much speculation over dinner later that evening.
Did Eric seem upset? Did he enjoy his stay?
Would we ever hear from him again?

An uncomfortable feeling hung in the air,
like something unfinished, unresolved.
It bothered us for hours, or at least until one
of us discovered what was in the pantry.

Go and see for yourself. It's still there after all these years, thriving in the darkness. It's the first thing we show any new visitors to our house. "Look at what our foreign exchange student left for us," we tell them.

"It must be a cultural thing," says Mum.

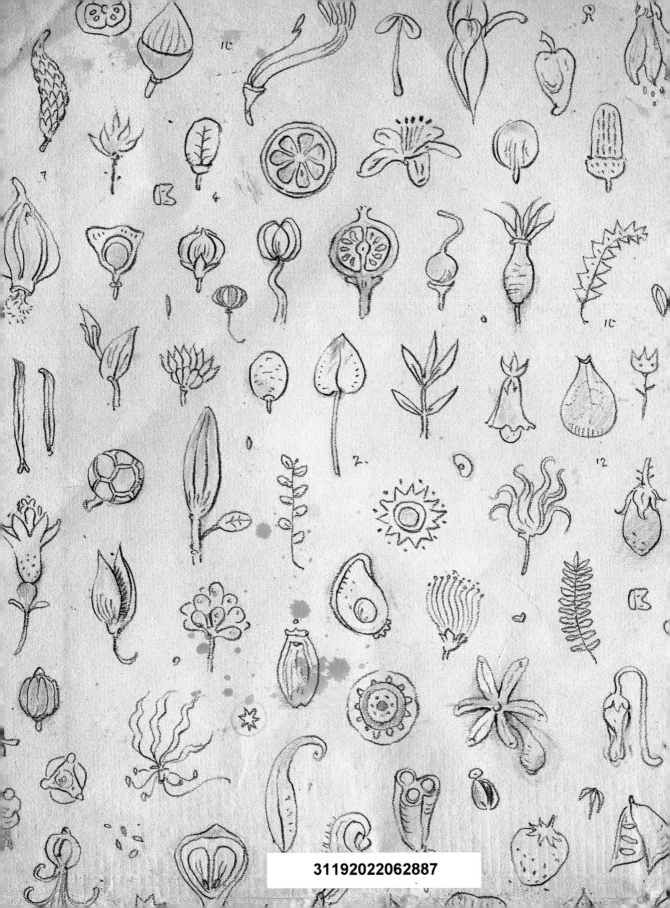